D0574857

Grey Mouse

Anke de Vries

ILLUSTRATIONS BY
Willemien Min

Front Street ℓ Lemniscaat
Asheville, North Carolina

One day, Grey Mouse felt blue.
She was bored and lonely.
And she was tired of being grey.

So she chose a bright color to cheer herself up.

"Maybe Goose will play with me now,"
Grey Mouse thought.
But Goose just giggled.

Grey Mouse tried green,
but Frog laughed loudly.

"Yellow is *not* a happy color,"
Grey Mouse decided.

"Maybe polka dots will work?"
But the ladybugs flew away.

Stripes felt silly when Zebra started to snicker.

Finally, Grey Mouse tried flowers.
And the bees did not laugh or fly away...

They flew straight toward her!
buzzzzzzz ... buzzzzzzz ...
Grey Mouse ran as fast as she could ...

... right into the water.

The bees were gone,
but Grey Mouse was greyer than ever
and just as blue.

"Hi," said a squeaky little voice.

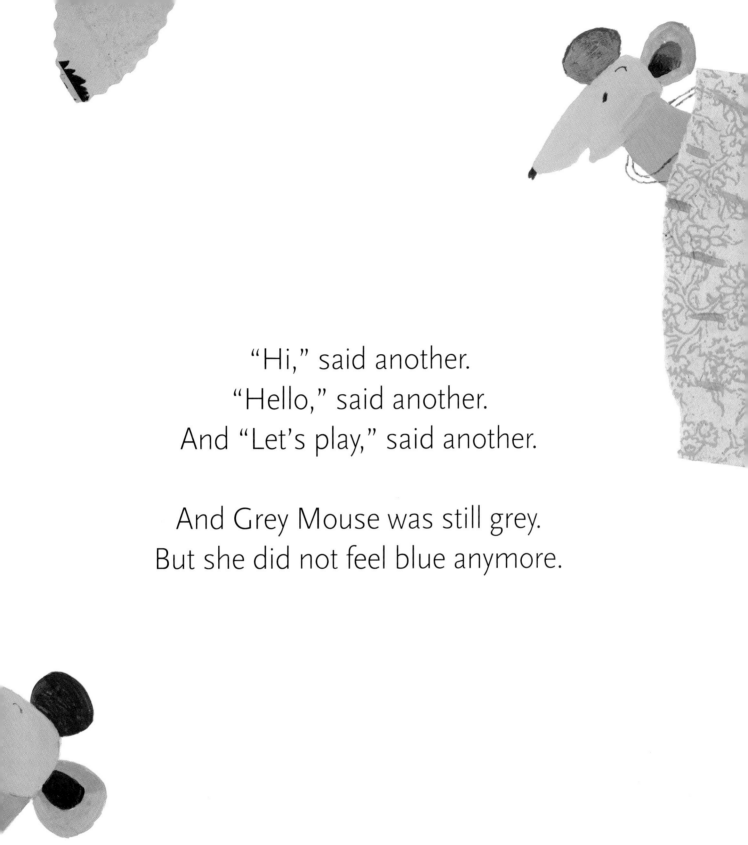

"Hi," said another.
"Hello," said another.
And "Let's play," said another.

And Grey Mouse was still grey.
But she did not feel blue anymore.